Heather

LINDA MAE PITMON

ISBN 978-1-0980-9237-5 (paperback)
ISBN 978-1-0980-9238-2 (digital)

Christian Faith Publishing, Inc.
832 Park Avenue
Meadville, PA 16335
www.christianfaithpublishing.com

Printed in the United States of America

Contents

Chapter 1

The New Owners

Heather rolled over on her back, basking in the warm sunlight that poured through the tall windows in the living room of the stately old house. She loved the big house with all the nooks and crannies that held excitement, mystery, and hiding places for every waking moment.

When she was young, she would crouch low between the large overstuffed chair and the oak end table, ready to pounce on anything that moved. Her back hair would stand straight up in anticipation of the innocent prey that would wander aimlessly into her clutch. Dreams of yesteryear that seem like a cloak of warmth on a winter day filled her empty moments with love.

Sharp, angry voices shouted orders that brought her quickly back into the bleak reality of today. Daylight had just broken, but the people who lived here were anxious to get things together and leave.

They usually slept until almost noon and stay three or four days. Now, they were screaming about being on time today, somewhere. Heather cowered back under the furniture and started to make her way back to the closet or down into the basement, whichever was the safest. She just knew that she should never be found here.

She had been foolish to lie in the living room to start with. These people hated everyone, including each other. *If they catch me in the living room, or anywhere inside or outside of the house, they…*

She didn't have time to finish her thought. Heather's quick thinking flashed across her brain because of the fear it brought.

Why they stayed together, she didn't know. Quietly as she could, Heather crept around the corner. Joan slung a red high-heeled shoe down the hallway at one of the men, just barely missing his head, landing with a sharp thud against the wall. It then fell to the floor next to Heather. The man quickly grabbed a small silver object from the small table above Heather and threatened to use it if she did it again.

"I don't care who you are. Dead is dead," he threatened in an angry voice.

"Cat hair all over my clothes again," Joan yelled. "If I find that animal, I'm killing it myself."

Heather tried to hide under the small table in the hallway as far against the wall as she could until the shouting hopefully would calm down. The man they called Jack tripped over the clutter and trash strewn through the front of the house, near the front door, and then he landed directly onto Heather's tail. Heather bit hard to swallow the pain without screaming.

If they knew she was in the house, it would be disastrous for her. Barely catching himself against the door, Jack yelled into Joan's face, returning hate for hate. Heather's nerves felt like fire from the pain in her tail. It throbbed without mercy.

She had just wanted to feel the security of her past, but it was anything but secure now. The fighting intensified. Just as quickly as they came yesterday, they rushed out the door and into their car, slamming doors and yelling the entire time.

Heather sighed from relief, even though the pain in her tail pierced her body. Them leaving just after coming yesterday was strange behavior, but she was grateful and thankful for it. They usually came in every few weeks so she could enjoy what time she had alone.

Heather decided to use the time to regain her self-respect and security. If she could have some routine to her day, maybe she would feel better. She had done so many things with Susan to pass the days in love and play. Even when Susan was in school, the evenings were filled with happiness.

Now, mostly, she pounced on her yarn ball that gave way to endless frayed strings, twitching ever so lightly in the breeze that flowed through the wide cracks in the floor and broken windows of the old home. Everything precious to her had been stripped away and thrown into the burning heap outside. A sense of blackness crept deep into her soul.

The house had been grand in its day. Two stories, the upstairs rooms and an old spooky basement, provided for many hours of investigation. The downstairs kitchen was in the back corner of the house. It had light honey-oak wainscoting on the walls, with a vinyl wallpaper above it that held small blue delicate flowers in a misty green field. The meadows were as delicate as the flowers captured within them.

There were three doors in the kitchen. One solid oak door led outside to the old porch in the back, and the other two light doors completed a circle path that led through the dining room, past the sitting room, rounding into the living room, down the stretch in the hallway, and back to the kitchen. The inside doors had been wedged open with small triangular stops under them to let the air flow through the house.

The fun of running through the downstairs was going from the blue carpeting of the hallway, living room and sitting room, to the slick oak-wood floors of the dining room and around to the yellow and blue linoleum on the kitchen floor, trying not to wipe out on the turns. Getting a foothold on the carpeting and tight turns through these rooms was a breeze. The smooth floors of the kitchen provided the challenge.

Trying to knock the multicolored yarn ball ahead of you was the exercise for the early morning. Susan had given Heather the yarn ball when she was young. It was wrapped up carefully and tightly, with all the various colors of yarn pieces that Susan's mother had given her from the knitting basket that sat next to the chair in the living room. Susan was proud of the ball when she had given it to Heather. Now it was frayed into pieces on the outside from lots of play, but it still held a close place in Heather's heart, like the raveled faded memories of Susan and the times gone by.

The upstairs was mostly bedrooms and baths. Heather never went up the stairs but at night. She used to sleep on the end of Susan's pink canopy bed. The room was decorated in delicate soft pink and lilac flowers. The wallpaper was full of roses and country homes. The floor was carpeted with plush lilac that felt warm when you first got up on a cold, winter morning. The curtains were white lace, pulled back with satin ties that gave an elegance to the room.

Susan had put her stuffed animals into a large overstuffed chair. Susan would hide beneath them, and Heather would set off to find her. Heather would dig through the animals, knocking them to the floor until Susan would reach up and grab her. Both Heather and Susan would roll onto the floor, Susan laughing and Heather purring loudly.

At first light, Heather would stretch out all her muscles until they couldn't go another inch, roll all the way over, and then get up. She would then rub against Susan's hand until she woke up, enough to give Heather a good rub down. Susan would then rub Heather's stomach, and Heather would lightly nip at Susan's fingers. They would play like this for ten minutes or so before Susan's mother would call them down for breakfast. They both would descend the stairs together. This had been the routine for Heather's first six months.

Now, only the blurred dream remained in the reality of a hungry tomorrow. A sharp chill rippled down Heather's back, and her mind went blank in defense. The empty cold of the house bit hard on Heather's stomach now. The fairy tale was passing more like a pleasant dream against the bleak reality of today. A whole year of a living nightmare was more than she had been ready for. She knew what living paw to mouth was. There was never enough food, never enough warmth, and never enough love to ease the soul's heart.

Heather decided to play with the ball of yarn this morning, trying to drive the bite of hunger from her stomach. She had hidden it carefully in the hall closet. The people who own the house now would never permit the yarn ball, or anything else that belonged to Heather, in the house.

The closet door, like the rest of the doors in the house, would no longer close tightly. The moisture and lack of heat had caused them to warp. The people didn't heat the house except when the temperature fell below fifty degrees. They said this old house, with its high ceilings and large rooms, took too much money to heat and do proper upkeep. Of course, they didn't stay here but on the first weekend of every month. It did not seem right, but Heather was almost more thankful when they were not here.

Even the smooth wood floor was no longer a challenge. The small boards had not been cleaned or repaired since Susan and her mother had moved. The yarn ball would catch on the snags in the floor as she tried to push it ahead of her. Now, she only played with it in the living room where the floor was covered with a flat ugly carpet that had not been vacuumed since the new owners put it down.

The ball was just behind an empty box in the closet. Heather took it out to the living room and rolled it in and out of the old couch and chair legs. *They were placed there for looks anyway*, thought Heather. They brought only enough furniture with them for the living room, some kitchen things, and one bed in each upstairs room.

Heather was afraid to go into the bedrooms when they were here. The first time she went in to sleep on the end of Joan's bed, she had been tossed all the way down the front stairs. Never would she do that again. She had ached for weeks recovering from the fall.

The ball of yarn kept her busy for an hour until she grew tired. Carefully, she placed the yarn ball back in the closet behind the empty box. Heather never knew when they would come now. They had never stayed for more than just a day or two before. She knew nothing would be left if it were in their sight. They never moved anything around unless they stepped on it anyway, so this was out of their way and their sight.

It seemed like the less food she got, the more tired she grew. She needed more sleep, both to rest the body and escape the reality of life. She played less nowadays as the energy of life faded like her dreams. All her energy had to be used searching for small scraps of food. Bits of playtime were precious indeed.

Like all the doors in the house that were warped and cracked, the crack in the back-basement door had provided her with the way in and out of the old house. She slipped out to the old car tire that rested in the back of the house, at the end of the driveway, near the small shed.

Heather fell asleep quickly even without food. She decided that she would get up later and forge through the thick tangled forest that encircled her home and, perhaps, wander to the outer edge of the woods where there were several other houses. There, she would find small scraps of food in the large silver garbage cans behind the houses near the city. Sometimes, a dog would chase her away, but it was better than starving.

One time, in the middle of last winter, she had been hit by a car, trying to avoid being lunch for a large brown boxer that discovered her in the garbage can. She had been so busy digging in the garbage can to uncover tidbits of nourishment that she had forgotten to listen for danger.

Eye to eye, a large boxer had cornered her in the can. He was stocky built, with smooth brown fur that was well cared for. After several minutes of barking and growling, Heather made the lunge for a getaway through the clumsy feet of the boxer. His sharp teeth had pierced the back flank of Heather's fragile body on both sides and ripped a huge gaping hole in her hip.

Nonetheless, she mangled a fair fight to get to freedom across a busy icy street nearby, meeting death at the roll of the car tires that sailed past her ears and across her tail nearly severing it. She had managed to get back to the edge of the forest where she lost consciousness. She didn't know how long she lay in the freezing snow. When she got up, there was still lots of pain in her hips and tail, but it had eased a little since the winter had passed.

Chapter 2

---- ✑ ----

The Quick Return

The familiar sound of the silver car came flying up the driveway and coming to a screeching halt. Heather tensed every muscle and then slowly edged up, carefully peeking above the rim of the tire just to get confirmation of the scene that she had visualized in her mind.

Why did they return so quickly? Heather wondered. They had never returned the same day as they left. If someone went to town for groceries or to pay bills, all the others stayed at the house. This was truly out of the ordinary and worried Heather.

"After you paint the car, then get it out of sight!" yelled Joe, a tall, slender man. He had deep-set brown eyes and dark-brown hair that was well-kept. "Don't want someone to see it before it's painted."

"Why don't you do it?" argued Jack. Jack was shorter and stocky built, with a ruddy face. He had light-brown hair that was always flying in all directions and around his face. "We will paint it later. I need to get this out of sight for now. Give me your guns. I'll hide them at the same time." He held a cloth bag that seemed to hold something important. He collected the guns from both the others and put them in another bag that looked like the first.

"Tell Joan to get the tarp all the way over that car and put hay on top of it for now. Don't let anyone have a reason to be snooping around here!" Jack yelled back at Joe and then turned angrily back toward the house.

All the while, the running and confusion scared Heather. She crouched low and as tight as she could get into the back and against one side of the tire. Joan was deliberately arrogant and haughty when she appeared at the door. She was never in a hurry and always wanted one of the men to wait on her to bring her everything she demanded. Heather had never seen her prepare a meal or clean the house. In fact, Heather had never seen her do anything but eat, scream, and demand everything.

Joe always microwaved the pizzas, at least that's what they ate most of the time anyway, and the aluminum cans they drank from, opened with a snap. *Not much to their mealtime, or to their lives,* thought Heather.

Joan slowly entered the house and slammed the heavy oak door with a thud behind her, which bounced back open again. Jack ran in after her swinging the door wide open and yelling. Patience wasn't one of their gifts on a good day, but today seemed to be very different and provided more irrational behavior than before. When Jack came out a few minutes later, he didn't have the bags or the guns either.

Heather's hair stood on end, even as she pushed her body tightly against the bottom edge of the tire. Maybe if she were invisible, the anger would pass, and things would begin to return to normal. The burning pain of their anger could fill her body and mind. It was the suffocating anger, even without them here, that touched her again and again.

Joe was busy pushing everything out of the way in the shed so the car would fit in. "Sure glad this isn't any smaller. The car wouldn't fit in otherwise!" Joe yelled. "You're supposed to know what you're doing anyway. Just like this morning, nothing. 'Do your job! Do your job!' You're always yelling. Now, because of you, we have nothing."

By this time, Jack was pulling the car in the shed, scraping the side on a metal hinge that had rusted and swung loose. "Can't even drive the car right!" Joe yelled.

"Shut up!" Jack screamed back. "How was I to know that today was different. I just don't understand. Why today? A year's worth of work down the drain," he moaned. "Just cover over the car and shut up."

Joe covered the car with the big ugly tan tarps he had thrown on the back porch earlier that summer. The tarps had molded after several rains, and the smell permeated the air with a pungent order. Dust flew like clouds bellowing before a thunderstorm.

Several times, they tripped over the old tire, where Heather cowered in fright. The angry screaming always scared her. These people scared her to begin with, and the violence had filled her life, but where else could she go? This was home, and maybe this was the way things were supposed to be. Heather had nothing to defend herself with.

As they finished putting the hay over the tarp, Joe jumped onto the porch and dashed into the house. "Sure hope there's food in there. I'm starved," Joe said. "It's going to be a long haul on nothing. Hope you have some other money stashed somewhere to wait this one out."

Jack just cringed, kicking the tire where Heather was hiding. The tire bolted into the air, rolling it and Heather, end over end and against the house with a sharp thud. Heather shot out of the tire like a rocket and hid in the overgrown weeds near the door of the basement until things grew quiet inside.

Heather crept into the basement and up the stairs very quietly. Step-by-step she was careful not to bump into anything or step where it would squeak. She had forgotten her hunger while all the commotion was stirring outside, but now the pain was strong and sharp in her.

"In the fridge," Joe said, sitting down on the couch beside Joan. "Get it yourself. I'm just as tired as you."

Jack laid his pizza on the arm of the chair and wandered out to the kitchen and opened the refrigerator. "Who's going to the store? We're almost out of everything."

"We're going to have to get things straightened out here first anyway, in case someone comes. You know, who's who. This is supposed to be a family, remember? A family with an elderly grandfather." Looking out to Jack in the kitchen, Joe quickly added, "By the way, you did get the makeup and stuff, didn't you?"

"Upstairs in the bedroom, like it's supposed to be," Jack snorted back over a can he took out from the refrigerator and slammed the door shut. After gulping down several swallows of the drink, he returned to the living room, still sulking. "Try to do a job right, and now faking it out like a family for nothing."

"Well, it's over now. We'll have to sit this one out until spring. Can't have anyone suspicious. Trying to act like a regular family and go to town for groceries at least until all of this blows over," Joe mumbled.

As Jack plopped back down, the pizza slipped from the arm of the chair to the floor. "Can't you do anything right!" Joe yelled.

"I didn't do it," Jack hollered.

Quickly, both men were up on their feet, yelling into each other's face. Heather saw her chance for food and dashed out from under the chair, snatched the pizza, and dragged it to the edge of the room where she thought she was safe.

Food, it felt so good in her mouth. The aroma had been enough to bring the saliva into her mouth long ago. Heather didn't wait to chew but gulped down several small bites of the pizza. She had just choked down the last bite when the pain of Jack's pointed-toe boot met with her side. "Stupid cat! Whose idea was it to keep her anyway?"

Heather gasped for breath and tried to keep the nauseous feeling from filling her mind. There was far more at stake here than just hope. It was survival now.

Joan jumped from the couch and yelled, "Get that cat out of here! Always hated them! Never any manners." Pointing her finger at Joe, she said, "You agreed to take care of that, that stupid thing. Get it out."

"Just a cat," Joe muttered. "Got the house cheaper with it anyway." Joe turned to leave the room when Jack lunged at Heather with his hand grabbing the back paw. Heather squirmed and meowed with a weak plea for help but was too weak to fight. He flung Heather out the back door so hard she hit the shed. The wind was knocked out of her, and mercifully, she eased into unconsciousness. Blackness filled her complete thoughts.

Chapter 3

———— ❧ ————

The Hole

S he lay there until the morning hours, trying to regain consciousness and enough of her strength to move away from the battle
zone again.

As Heather lay there, she tried to remember the way it was
before. Heather was torn between the survival of now and the
wounded memory of the past. The stately old home rested on several
acres of thick-wooded forest that surrounded it. The house had been
painted a rich dusty blue with white window shutters that were now
hanging by one hinge or torn down by the wind and neglect. The
paint had peeled, giving it an appearance of the bark of a tree rolling
up and falling to the ground. The wind and rain faded the color to
more of a dirty gray and blue.

The house had a small shed, just big enough for Susan's parents
to park the car. It was both security and protection to keep the limbs
that were blown from the huge oak trees from falling on the car
during a storm. The small shed had been painted to match the house,
with white trim accenting the doors.

Now, the sides of the shed had been hit so many times by
the stranger's car it no longer stood but leaned beside the house in
despair. The house and shed gave an aura of complete abandonment.
Heather guessed that if they didn't take care of these things, they
wouldn't want a useless cat either. Both seem to feel weary and tired.
The house was a short distance in the country. The woods that sur-

rounded the house was mixed with tall white oaks and maple trees. The sprinkling of pink and white dogwood trees would always welcome the spring. Red trees lined the driveway, all the way to the highway on the backside away from the city.

After the strangers moved in, Heather found an old tire that had been tossed aside near the shed, at the end of the driveway. It was usually out of the war zone. She had pulled a piece of torn cloth from the trash one afternoon when everyone was gone. She felt at least somewhat safer outside than inside now, while the people were here. She had a fair chance to make a getaway, at least until the other afternoon. Only when hunger or nostalgia drove her back inside would she move to the stench of the house.

Hunger still plagued her to find something to eat. She started wandering slowly down the small path toward the edge of the city to find food. It was a long way in her weakened state, and Heather had to stop several times to catch her breath. The pain was sharp in her side and plunged deep inside when she walked, or even when she took a breath.

As Heather neared the edge of the forest, she grew more careful. *Don't trust anyone*, she thought. Carefully and quietly, she veered to the left this time. *Maybe more food down this way*, she mused. This was the first time she ventured in the direction, and maybe she would find more food here, or safer territory away from the dogs.

An alley with several cans caught her eye. Heather could almost taste morsels; she was so hungry. Quietly, she jumped to the first can and found some dry moldy bread. "Can't be choosy now," she said as she gulped the food down quickly. The next house had more to offer. Fish smells permeated the air, and Heather almost fainted from the overwhelming odor. Quickly, she grabbed two bites and downed them without chewing. She choked as they stuck in her throat, but she mustered enough strength to swallow. She took the next few bites slower. Still, the hunger drove her to eat as fast as she could.

As she finished, sleep became the driving instinct. She found a small towel that had been thrown next to the trash in a private corner, where she wouldn't be discovered. After turning around a few times to see which was the best way to lie down, she collapsed into a deep restful sleep, filled with feline nightmares.

The sun glittered through the trees, stroking Heather's fur in a gentle breeze of angel hands trying to heal the fragile spirit that had been crushed. Heather tossed and turned, fighting the demons in her mind.

Several minutes later, Heather was wakened to the soft voice of a small girl. She was in a small playhouse behind the big house, talking to her doll. "Take a nap now," she said quietly. "I'll rock you to sleep with a lullaby." The small girl sang to her doll while rocking for several minutes. She was a little younger than she remembered Susan. A great loneliness surrounded Heather's heart. If a cat could cry, Heather did.

Several children joined the small girl. Her home had a warm friendly glow and the feeling of a gentle love surrounding it. There was a large backyard that had several playthings strewn around. The house was a bilevel, with a large garage attached on the side. It was painted green, with white trim on the windows and doors.

The small girl and her friends disappeared inside the house, only to reappear in the upstairs window. *That must be her room,* thought Heather.

The little girl soon got tired of the games. She walked toward the window and began gazing out into the yard. The little girl's eyes seem to be fixed in a hypnotic gaze. Heather thought she must be dreaming of someone, or something, she left behind. Heather knew that feeling well. The girl's intense look made her remain quite still, as if watching something. Although the pain still grasped her from the inside, Heather twitched her tail in excitement.

I wonder what she sees? Heather questioned her own mind. She let her thoughts wander back to Susan. Both girls had long straight blonde hair. Susan had hers put into a single ponytail that danced and played as she ran. This girl wore hers straight as it flowed to the center of her back. Heather couldn't see the girl's eyes but knew that they had to be the blue of the sky, like Susan's.

The little girl had called an adult to the window and both stared out the window intently. *This must be her mother, like Susan's mother.*

Heather felt the commotion began to bring the old fear of strange people back.

Heather's stomach turned and tightened. Quickly, she darted back down the alley to the familiar safety of the woods. She thought she could hear someone calling her from behind. A terrible fear pushed its way into Heather's mind that taunted her hopes. Reality told her she didn't want to feel new blows of pain from raiding the garbage.

The fish from the garbage had filled her enough so she didn't feel the pain of hunger, but the pain in her ribs throbbed from running. She slowed to a walk, and then the emptiness of home began to creep into her heart. Going home didn't bring excitement but an empty heaviness. Heather felt completely lost, never belonging anywhere. This was her house, but not her home anymore. Loneliness crept over her life, like the evening shadows swallow the day into a deep abyss.

Sneaking in through the ragged crack in the basement door, Heather decided to see how things were. She felt the presence of the people before she saw them. The liquid they drank had a foul odor, and it floated heavily in the air. They had passed out where they were. At least, for now, they would leave her alone, and she could find some small bits and pieces of food to eat now and keep her hunger at bay for a few more hours.

Hunger had driven her to eat as much as she could for times when the people were not around to supply the small crumbs and garbage. Rummaging for food from the kitchen was no-easy task, even now. Heather would have to drag the pieces she could carry through the hall, down the stairs, up the basement stairs, squeeze through the door, and out to the shed for each piece. She knew if she didn't, there might not be any food later. Starvation was always standing in her shadow. When these people disappeared, they would be gone for maybe three or four weeks.

Carefully, she began the long task, picking up the dry crust from beside the chair. Quickly as she could, she scurried down the hall to the door, down the steps to the basement, up the steps, through the crack, and out to the shed. *To the shed,* she thought. *No, they have taken over the shed.*

Heather looked around and decided that now, the tire wasn't a very safe place either. Quickly, she took the food down to the basement. *Maybe a corner of the old cellar.* She remembered the times when Susan's mom used to store food here. She had a small vegetable garden out beside the old shed in the summer.

Heather quickly crept into the cellar. The cobwebs had taken over most of the shelves. Only a few broken jars remained on the shelves and the floor near the back corner. *This is it,* thought Heather. *There isn't any other safe place. The only time these people come down here was to dig a small hole in the back of this room.*

As Heather looked up, she realized the hole had just been recently covered with a board from the broken storage shelves. They sure didn't have the upkeep of the house in mind, as now there were broken shelves to add to the broken windows and doors. It seemed like they were deliberately destroying everything, including Heather's memories.

The small windows of the top edge of the basement wall were very dirty and only allowed tiny bits of the afternoon sunlight to enter, and the dust from neglect streamed through the air, allowing the sunlight to dance on the floor, like fairy dust in the breeze.

Heather turned around just in time to hear Joan and Jack stumbling and tripping down the steps. Still consumed in their world after a day of drinking, their feet tempted to go their own way and not always where they wanted them. Heather hid behind the jars, crouched into the smallest wad she could make.

Joan was going to inspect some work that Jack was finishing down here. *That hole,* she thought. *That stupid hole.*

Heather didn't care. Wasn't there anywhere safe from them? They pushed open the door to the cellar and argued about the hole that was covered. Joan argued that the plaster he bought won't look old enough to be part of the original wall if someone came snooping around.

Who would want to come here? Heather sneered to herself.

Jack yelled back, "Just smear some dirt on it, and it'll be okay! I can't go into town now and buy anything else like that. That would really give us away."

Jack could not seem to stand straight on his feet or control the direction of his fall. He fell into Joan, and they both caught hold of the shelf standing in the front of the room, spilling the broken jars everywhere.

Then Heather made her get away just in time for Jack to laugh and lunge toward her. His pointed-toe boot caught Heather again. Heather didn't know when she woke up or what happened. She only knew something had to change.

Chapter 4

— ✑ —

The Mouse

That night, Heather slept in the tree trunk that had rotted out at the edge of the forest. At least the rotted wood provided a soft bed for her weary body. She dug out a small area, just big enough for her to lie down in at the back edge. Then she circled the bed, pressing everything in place and then collapsed.

Every time they came, it was the same story. They would kick her and throw her until being unconscious was a generous blessing to her. *How can they be any different?* Heather wondered. *Maybe I'm not good enough for them. Maybe I'm just stupid. Besides, where can I go that is any different? Wherever I go, it seems to be the same.* Somewhere in her despair, Heather slept.

The cold night air would make for painfully stiff joints and muscles the next morning, but for tonight, sleep was her blanket of love. Heather dreamed of the first owners of the old home.

Heather had been born in this house and was at least happy for the first six months. Then they sold the house to the present owners and moved to Hartford, Connecticut. Susan's mother had taken a position with an insurance firm there after Susan's father died last year.

Last year had been tough. No one took care of Heather, and she began to doubt her abilities to take care of herself now. There was never anyone to feed her or brush her fur like Susan, the little girl did. Oh, how Heather missed the time when Susan would spend the afternoon playing in the yard, pulling a small toy mouse through the grass for Heather to pounce on. She felt a twinge of homesickness in her stomach. "No use dreaming of foolish things!" she chided herself. "What's gone is gone."

The reality of the morning came with hunger pains again. A cold drizzle of rain had fallen during the night, giving the yard a sheen, like a mirror. The mist from the rain was cold, and Heather was shivering inside and out. The sun would not warm the ground today, and Heather knew that winter was coming quickly. The short days and long nights brought a shudder through Heather's heart that would not stop.

This was the same time of year that Susan and her mother left. The winter that followed seemed like a dismal nightmare. Several people had been here to see the old house, and a tall gentleman had shown them through the home, pointing out the beautiful warm woodwork and high ceilings. A grand old home with two stories and a basement.

"I'll bet this is a bear to heat." seem to be the only answer that came from most of the people. They didn't seem to finish the tour before they left. Not one seemed to stop and pet Heather. She desperately needed to feel the touch of a soft, tender hand scratching her back and under her chin. Heather had given up, hoping for an owner to buy the place until one afternoon. The man selling the house had barely said two words until the man said, "Looks like the perfect set up. Real, real secluded. Don't like visitors, grandfathers. You know how they are," he added quickly. Doesn't like visitors much since he's grown older. Makes him nervous."

"The cat goes with the house," the salesman said quickly. "The seller couldn't take her. Said the city was no place for this free spirit. Made me promise to take care of her and have the new people know she comes with the house. There is a small amount of money set aside for food if you take the house. Felt sorry for the little girl though. They were friends, good friends."

"Don't make me any difference, with or without. Write your check tomorrow morning. See you at the office at nine." With that, they were quickly gone.

The excitement swelled inside Heather. A new family, maybe another girl or an older grandfather, that would like to just have someone to keep him or her company would be nice. All evening, she washed and arranged her fur with a musical purr, dancing in her mind. Tomorrow was to be a new beginning.

The next day, about noon, they came. No grandfather, just two men and a lady. *Oh, well*, thought Heather. *Maybe they need a friend.* Heather slid up to the legs of the lady in the kitchen, putting away a few things. An awful screech pierced the air, and the nap of fur on Heather's back stood straight up in the air. Heather darted through the door and hid in a box that was left on the porch.

"What happened?" asked the tall slender man running as if to rescue a damsel in distress.

"Cat!" screamed the lady.

"Oh, forget the cat and put away the things so it looks like were living here. Salesman said it came with the territory. Maybe if you will ignore it, it will find another home. Just don't feed it. I don't want you wasting our money on that stupid thing."

"Don't need to worry about that!" the woman yelled back. "I hate cats anyway."

The year that followed was long, cold, and empty. Heather had never known someone to kick her, but that winter, she felt the hard toe of several shoes.

There was never any food or water left out in her small dish at the end of the counter. In fact, the dish was thrown into the trash. Heather had knocked over the trash to retrieve the small heart-shaped bowl that Susan had given her just before she left. When Jack found the small bowl in the corner of the kitchen, he had taken the heel of his shoe and smashed it to bits.

That first night when the woman they called Joan came back from grocery shopping, she kicked Heather across the room. Heather tried as she could to show her the friendship Susan would have cherished. After each of the first blows, Heather laid for several minutes, without knowing what had happened, or why.

Finally pulling herself into a conscious position after several sharp blows, she heard Joan yelling and screaming. One man quickly grabbed Heather, opened the door, and threw her into the cold yard, where she lay the rest of the night. This was only the beginning of her nightmares.

It hurt to move the next day, and it was several weeks before Heather even ventured near the kitchen again. She banished herself to the rubbish heap in the backyard, where they sometimes threw the trash. At the end of the day, she would relegate herself to the shed that held some loose hay that made a warm bed.

And then, they left as quickly as they came. Heather thought she might have other people looking to buy the home, but every three weeks, the same people came back for the weekend. Usually, they stayed about three or four days, and then they disappeared again as quickly as they came.

The house deteriorated from a grand old home to just an old house. The people never seem to care if trash was strewn in or out of the house. They just live there once in a while, practicing with things they called guns in the back of the house, against the shed.

By now, the house and shed were weather beaten, and the broken windows were taped with cardboard. The trash heap in the backyard was infested with mice and rats. Loose papers had blown all over the yard and, when the rain came, it glued them to wherever they landed at the time.

Heather began wandering farther and farther from the old home just to survive. During the fall, the forest mice had provided several treats to keep her alive. She never had to catch mice before Susan left. Now, she had gotten quite good at pouncing from an immovable silence into a whirlwind of fur.

One time, while the people were gone, Heather had dared to catch a small gray mouse in the kitchen. While she was eating the small morsel, another mouse ran into her quite by accident. Both mouse and Heather had collapsed in terror and surprise, but Heather had recovered quickly, and the feline instinct controlled her every move. Not really wanting two mice for lunch, Heather had left it in the middle of the kitchen floor for the next day.

That afternoon, the people had come in for their once-a-month stay. Joan swept into the house, as usual, like a royal princess. She demanded this and that from anyone that was near enough to hear. Heather was listening quietly from the hall closet, where she had been playing with her yarn ball. After she had hidden the yarn ball back in the corner of the closet, quietly, Heather looked down the hall and back to the basement stairs to leave through the basement door.

Barely had she reached the bottom of the stairs, when a piercing scream of terror had reached the roof and shattered the nerves of everyone in the house. When Joan came into the house that evening, she slipped her shoes off to be more comfortable. Joan stepped on the soft furry gray mouse. After she realized what was under her foot, she ripped through the house and out the front door, to collapse in the car. A chuckle of welcome delight passed through Heather when she realized that she had been the cause of the immediate episode and had pulled it off without becoming the blunt of their cruelty.

Only one man stayed in the house that night, with an all-out vengeance to rid the house of mice. Every corner of the downstairs and basement had a trap. Poison was placed in packets under the cabinets, around the basement steps, and everywhere else they couldn't reach to place a trap.

Heather's mouse had given Joan quite a scare, and Heather felt a warm glow of being the source of that. Maybe some of her new skills have been good for Heather to have.

Chapter 5

—— ✺ ——

The Girl

As the weather worsened, Heather had to go farther and farther into the woods as the mice went underground to keep warm during the winter. The house contained the poison, and the mice that ate the poison were just as dangerous. It wasn't long before she discovered secret treasures hidden carefully in the garbage cans located in alleys behind the houses at the edge of the city.

Sneaking back in the house today had become the challenge, knowing when all the people would be asleep. After a long night of partying, she thought, no one would be awake this morning. This had been their routine every time they came. Over the house came the stench of alcohol and smoke. *You didn't need to worry about making a little noise now,* Heather thought.

The people seem like limp rags thrown over the couch, chair, and beds. Joan stirred a little in the upstairs bedroom, moaning about a severe headache, but fell back into the pillow. Heather didn't think she would move from there for a little while. It might give her a little time.

Still, Heather was careful not to create any noise. The fear of being caught by these people still pierced her body. Just the thought of it brought the fur on Heather's back straight up in the air. After yesterday, when Heather thought they would not stir and found her in the basement, brought sharp pain back into her agonizing reality.

As she silently tiptoed through the house, she knew the party had been just for drinking. There wasn't any food laying on the table. The dry crumbs had been there for several days, and only the mice would have been tempted to lick them up from the floor for an appetizer. Cans lay everywhere, some standing and some laying sideways, spilling even a small amount of liquid flowing into the carpet.

Wandering back into the yard, the need for food pulled at Heather's insides. Just a little leftover pizza would've been enough to delay the pain until she could forage through the forest into the neighbor's garbage. This routine had not made the neighbors friendly, but a broom is better than starving.

Heather started down the path toward the town. She shook inside and trembled on the outside from hunger and neglect. Today was bitter. The cold air bit at her face. The twigs snapping sharply under her paws brought back memories of the days she could have pranced down through the woods without making a sound. Her body would've landed as light as a feather, but not today. She not only stumbled heavily down the path, but she did not care if she made a sound. Suddenly, Heather remembered the little girl at the edge of the forest. Going back to the girl's home brought a tinge of excitement and fear. The fear of being caught, since they already knew she had been there before, and the excitement of food tingled inside her. The memories of the past and seeing a reminder of Susan hastened her steps. Quickly, her step became a little lighter and a little softer.

Today, the girl played in the backyard with her toys. Her mother had bundled her up in a dark blue winter coat, and knitted hat, the whole works. She almost looked like Heather's ball of yarn. Heather chuckled inside as she watched the small girl maneuver around with all the winter wear.

As the girl waddled over to her playhouse, Heather caught her eye. The girl stopped quickly in her tracks and turned toward Heather, facing her eye to eye. Heather's green eyes must have been the size of silver dollars as she realized her dilemma. She stood frozen as a stone statue with the heightened alert of a bird, ready for flight to escape the calm reality.

Her mother came to the door when the girl softly called her. Fear began swelling in Heather's chest as her mother leaned out to see what the small girl was saying. "Come out here. She's here now." The girl tried to use a soft, gentle voice, but the excitement swelled inside, so even the bulkiness of her clothes showed the energy of her excitement building.

Heather grew more frightened with each word she said, but the eye-to-eye contact with the little girl held a spell as only Susan had done. Heather wanted Susan again, but the reality that she was gone forever loomed over her. She had not thought the strangers would have been like they were. Now, not knowing what to do, the hypnotic voice and soft blue eyes drew Heather's heart, but the fear and anxiety swelled in her chest, and then tightness in her throat choked her breath until she thought she would burst.

The girl eased slowly and quietly down on her knees and talked so softly. Heather's fur stood at total attention from her ears to the tip of her tail, and her knees locked stiff. The small girl eased a little closer and called, "Heather."

That's all it took. The fear exploded, and Heather blindly scrambled for the back alley in a panic.

Heather didn't know why the fear, excitement, and panic mixed like they did. Was she afraid this was a dream? Why did she call her name? Heather didn't know. She only wanted the safety of…what? She just ran.

Heather found the path through the woods and tore down the path, angry and terrified, with her claws tripping over the exposed tree roots on the path. The fear eased as Heather drew herself deeper into the woods and its blanketing silence. Besides having no food today, a new freezing rain had begun, and Heather was extremely tired. This whole day had exhausted the emotion and energy of three days.

Heather decided she would not go home, at least not for now. She needed a nap, but where was she to sleep outside was another hard decision. She had decided that the forest edge near the city was almost home and still away from home. She rummaged through the forest to find a place that would provide both safety and protection from the cold rain and from other dangers.

Heather decided that trash was a common part of her home now. Several old tires and trash bags have been discarded at the edge of the wooded area near the city. She scavenged through the bags of wet garbage to find protection from the cold rain. She had to dig deeper until she found enough dry rags out of the garbage to make a comfortable bed in an old rusty trash barrel. This was almost too good to be true. Heather decided a short nap was the thing to christen this as her new sleeping place.

After she woke from her nap, Heather stretched every muscle in her body. It really hurt, but it was the only way she could continue living. The aching deep in her soul grew more painful with each step in her life.

Heather slipped into the cold basement and up the stairs to see if the way was clear of trouble. They were still in the house, but a quiet silence of the cold, cloudy day seem to dominate even the human's thoughts. What Heather needed now was sleep and the security of Susan and her dream.

Softly, she crept out of the basement door into the hallway. She was too exhausted from hunger alone to stay too long listening for the battle cries. Stumbling quietly as she edged around the hallway through the warped door of the closet, Heather slipped quietly into the closet, behind the empty box to the soft yarn ball and curled tightly around it into the silence. Heather was aware of new bags in the closet but was too tired to investigate. As her eyelids slipped close and she surrendered to sleep, Heather felt the tickle of the frayed strings against her fur. Susan slipped into her heart, calming the thoughts of the weary cat. The darkness and terror of the night had been replaced by the warm glow of Susan, or the girl, or…the two meshed into one girl, and Heather slept.

By the middle of the night, loud angry voices came surprisingly clear. Heather knew it was trouble to be found in the house, but even more trouble to have them find the yarn ball and destroy the only security Heather knew. Heather pushed the yarn ball as far back into the closet corner as she could. Dust balls clung to the frayed ends.

She tried to listen and decide when they were far enough, away from the closet to make a hasty escape without being discovered, or at least caught. Footsteps and voices hassled back and forth, too near for Heather to make a break. Doors slammed and bounced open again as the tension and anger built to a peak.

Tonight was different somehow. The angry voices came earlier and louder than they had before. A small break in the sound came. Heather slipped quietly from the closet into the hall and started toward the basement door, when she thought the silence indicated they were far enough away to escape.

Heather almost made it to the basement door, but no farther. Joan leaned out of the kitchen door into the hallway so she could yell back at Jack when she spied the cat. Joan slammed the door from behind on Heather's side, crushing her thin ribs between the door and the door jam, giving her a renewed pain in her side.

Heather renewed her efforts to escape and leap down the basement steps. The scream of anger was as much toward Joe as it was toward Heather. "I told you to get rid of that!" Joan screamed. Then throwing the shoes she held down the stairs at Heather, and she slammed the door.

This was enough for Heather. Things were going to be different. She didn't know how, but she had to try. The short night sleep had eased very little of the pain of the last few days, but no one would stand against this each month. Heather knew her body would not survive this through the winter. During the summer, she could forage through the trash and stay in the woods, but the cold, icy winter brought about pain and hunger, as well as the need for shelter.

Heather returned to her new sleeping quarters to finish the night. At least Heather was warm here for tonight, cuddled deep in the rags, and Heather slept.

Chapter 6

―――――― ∽ ――――――

Rest for The Weary

Morning was brought on abruptly when a dog was nosing through the trash to discover if his breakfast was here. He was an old lame Irish Setter that had been abandoned years ago. His weather-beaten reddish-brown coat hung on his bones and had long since lost its sheen for life. His deep-brown eyes were empty, while his sniffing nose searched the rubbish heap, more out of ritual than anticipation. His movements paced from one bag to the next, confirming his knowledge of each container.

Heather had been in such a deep sleep, she had not heard his coming, and Heather had been so quiet, the dog did not know she was there. Complete isolation had consumed each in their own worlds.

They met nose to nose. Who was frighten the most? They didn't know. Eye to eye, Heather and her fur stood straight up in the air, and the old dog's legs were like Jell-O. Heather hissed and lashed the old dog's nose with her front paw. The old dog yelped painfully, trying to make his legs carry him in the opposite direction.

Tangled in his own back legs, the dog's clumsy body fell into a large green trash bag laying at the entrance to the barrel. Rotted garbage and crumpled paper flew everywhere, filling the air with the foul stench.

Heather scrambled outside and jumped to the top of the barrel for safety. The twig holding the barrel snapped under the weight and struggle from Heather and the dog, allowing it to start rolling quickly down the hill and over the trash bags toward the dog. The dog, Heather, and the barrel hit a small bump, causing them to tumble through the air into a ravine. When they landed, it was in the freezing creek at the bottom. The drenched dog yelped and limped away, with his tail between his legs and the smell of garbage soaked through his fur. The old dog began running for the safety of the city. Heather was soaked to the skin, hissed and tore off for the safety of the house. After a thorough shake to detach any remaining rubbish, or water, both dropped in their "homes" with strange worlds spinning in their heads and with wide eyes of wonderment.

As the terror was replaced by hunger, Heather decided to look for food as the morning brought on a cold emptiness back to her stomach. The path between her home and the alley, where the little girl lived, had an inviting warmth today. Although the air was nippy, the sun shone through the clouds for the first time since the new owners came this time. *Maybe an omen of good*, thought Heather. She needed something good today.

Her body and fur were dull and coarse because of the lack of nourishment and love, both inside and out. She no longer had a sheen of a golden yellow tabby fur in the sunlight, and the black tip of her tail almost blended with the mud. The white bib below her mouth no longer glisten but gave way to the dull dirty-matted fur that covered her body.

She no longer pranced with a light step, but the awkward movement of a broken spirit and neglected body and cruelty. You could hardly tell she had been a vibrant and beautiful kitten. Her green eyes held no hope for any revival now.

She was a bit more careful as she neared the area where she had been so notably introduced to the dog. No surprises like that twice in one day. A shiver went through her just at the thought. *Funny,* thought Heather now, *that he was just as scared, and what a site we both must have been.* She hummed a "purrrrr" that tickled her ears.

Just as she came to the edge of the wooded area, she spied the old Irish Setter tipping garbage containers in the alley to the right. Heather stopped and watched him for a few minutes. He was just as homeless as she was. An empty shell with saggy skin on top of bones and covered with dirty matted fur was what they had both become.

The old dog turned and faced Heather straight on. Neither seem to want to move, nor were either of them scared of each other as they had been this morning. Heather thought that they both longed for companionship but neither knew how to begin. Heather slowly turned to the left and started a little slower down the alley, while the old dog moved to the next trash can.

Suddenly, there was a loud crash. Several trash cans scattered like dominoes through the alley, spewing their contents. An adult came from the house where the old dog was, and another explosion, like the one from the house where they had been practicing with the guns, shattered the air. The old dog yelped painfully and limped into a run into the edge of the forest and disappeared.

Heather cowered down, almost too frightened to move, as she watched the scenes unfold like an old picture of the times past in her head. After a while, Heather gathered her wits and started out again.

It seemed automatic to take the left trail out of the forest into the alley behind the girl's home, but a small excitement began to fill her being. Maybe she could just watch the children for a while. She should be more careful not to be noticed today. At least she hadn't run into any dogs down this alley. People were a different story.

At the back of the house, Heather was taken by surprise and amazement to find a small dish of food placed at the side of the trash. The aroma delighted Heather's nose and brought back memories of a lost time. She pushed her nose down on the top of it to test it. It was beef flavored soft food. It was like someone left it here deliberately. Why these people left this out, Heather didn't know, and she didn't know if she really cared. It was real food, and Heather was hungry.

Scarfing down the food as fast as she could, Heather looked up now to see if anyone was coming, but everything was eerily quiet this morning. Heather checked the house to see if anyone had come outside. No one was near.

That's when Heather spied the girl in the window. She had been watching all the time, and her mother was in the shadow of the house, behind the girl. They made no moves to come out, or to bother her while she ate. It was almost as if they knew how hungry she was.

Heather continue eating at a slower pace. This was the first time in a long time. Heather didn't know that she was not gulping down the food in desperation, or running for her life. This was going to be Heather's day; she could feel it inside and began feeling a warm hope.

After the meal, Heather decided to sit at the edge of the yard and inspect the area. She sniffed around enough to know that this was a neighborhood of cats, not dogs. That was good enough for Heather. She would come this way more often. Even the people seemed more… No, Heather would never assume the best anymore.

Heather was quickly surprised and stopped abruptly when she saw the girl appeared at the back doorway. She had been so engrossed in the smells of the yard that she forgot to watch the door. The girl made no sound but just stood there, watching. Her mother joined her shortly, but neither came any nearer. Both stood abrupt and tall. A minute or so passed without any movement. Heather felt the time had come to leave before they did.

Heather paced her steps carefully so no sound came under her feet. If they followed her, it would only be by site and not by any sound she made. Almost relieved, she glanced over her shoulder, and no one was following.

Quickly, she ducked onto the path to the old house. A small weak whining distracted her concentration, and she decided to investigate the sound. As she edged toward the old garbage heap, Heather spotted the old Irish Setter laying limp at the edge of the garbage heap where they first met.

She carefully moved closer, paw over paw, until she realized that he was not going to make any moves toward her. He seemed to be in a lot of pain. As Heather drew closer, she could see the matted fur had a new addition of blood on his front shoulder.

He looked up slowly, and then closed his eyes again. Heather pushed her way up under his feet and curled into his body to give him what small amount of warmth and love she had left. Maybe it wasn't enough, but it was all she had.

The afternoon was almost over, and evening came quickly. Heather returned to the girl's house and found the bowl full again. This time, she savored the smell of chicken-flavored food. It was the dry and crunchy kind. At the edge was a small piece of yellow cheddar cheese. Heather could almost feel Susan's presence at the familiar routine.

The crunch was as sweet as the taste. She carefully ate all the food, without spilling it on the ground. After the rain, a couple of days ago, the ground was still wet. That would spoil the crunch and draw water from the oily driveway. Then it wouldn't be fit to eat. Heather left the cheese until last, her dessert. At first, she smelled it to savor the aroma. Then she licked it lightly, to bring her taste buds to the fullest delight. Then she ate the cheese.

Two meals in one day was unthinkable. She knew that these people had left it here for her. But Heather knew that people traps were extremely dangerous. They were watching from the house but never made a move. Heather was on alert and ready to run but somehow felt she could be at ease for the first time in a year.

Heather slipped quietly to the edge of the forest path, just inside where the evening sunlight had gently heated the leaves, making a warm, soft bed. The old dog had moved only a few feet before laying in a pile of maple leaves and resting quietly. He looks so tired and weary, but at least more comfortable now, at least not in as much pain. A strange deep bond had formed from necessity and provided her with something she needed and the old dog needed as well.

As she circled the chosen spot of leaves next to the old dog, she began fluffing and arranging her bed. Heather noticed a tint of color in the leaves, fluttering in the gentle breeze. Winter was gently creeping into her life but, for now, she lay next to the old dog and sleep crept over her eyes, and she fell asleep.

Chapter 7

——— ✑ ———

The Return

When she awoke, Heather felt a little hungry. She chuckled to herself, "a little hungry." She hadn't been a little hungry, it seemed forever. Even though the wet-matted fur, her bones were not as visible this morning, she knew that hunger was always knocking at her door.

She felt good this morning. As she left the old dog, he had not moved; his breathing was exceptionally light. *He would be all right here, and sleep is probably what he needs the most,* thought Heather. *Maybe later I will come and see how he is.*

She thought that this morning she would slip into the house, since she was here, to see if they had anything left out from the night before. Hunger still brought panic to her bones. She decided to sneak through the living room, when she didn't find anything in the kitchen. Nothing but glasses of bad tasting liquid and a few hard pizza crusts were scattered around the room. Heather nibbled at the crust but decided that there were better places to look today.

Heather crept back down the steps and through the crack in the door to go outside. She hadn't even noticed the crisp fresh fall air this morning. The sun was peeking through the leaves and dancing on the forest floor. The soft breeze and warm sunlight began drying her fur.

The trail back to the girl's house was easy to trace this morning. Heather had a quick light step that looked like she felt this morning.

As she passed the old dog, her steps softened and slowed to a full walk. Heather noticed that he had his eyes fixed on her. They were no longer empty but seemed to be filled with memories and times gone by. Heather, not wanting to intrude on his happiness, slipped on by leaving him to his memories.

This morning, fish-flavored soft foods filled the dish. It was delicious, and Heather savored it for a long time. She ate slowly so the flavor and the aroma would linger. Again, the fullness of Heather's stomach began to warm the feeling she had long forgotten or suppressed. She no longer cared if the girl watched her eat, as long as she didn't come near. She was ready to run but didn't feel the need would come. Still, she remained at attention with her fur tingling up and down her spine.

The girl had been sitting on the step of the house with something in her hands. Heather couldn't tell from here, but she must've had the same feeling about it that Heather had about the yarn ball. The girl watched the cat as she played with her toy. She cradled it carefully in her hand. As she held it up to talk to it, Heather saw that it was a doll.

"Susan," she said, "I told you I would take care of Cindy and watch that Heather was taken care of, and I have."

Who are all those people? thought Heather. *Why would anyone name someone else Heather? That's my name.*

Heather listened quietly for a while and then noticed a small bowl of water, clean, fresh water. She sniffed and delightfully washed down the last bite of her food. As Heather sat cleaning herself as best as she could, she thought she could handle anything today.

The girl continued to rock the doll and watch the cat. The soothing voice of the girl gently rocking the ragdoll brought back memories of Susan playing in her room just before bedtime with a doll she named Cindy. A new feeling of homesickness flowed over her.

Sitting quietly at the edge of the yard, she watched the little girl even more carefully. The girl never made quick moves or yelled, like the new owners of her home did.

Heather slipped her way back into the forest and quietly near the old dog. He still had not moved, and Heather became frightened.

As she crept closer, she could see that his eyes were again empty. This time, when she came closer, he was not breathing. The angel of death had rescued another from the clutches of the world.

Heather was both relieved and empty. They had formed a closeness in their lonely, empty worlds, and now she was totally alone again. Thankful for the time they had together and yet mourned his loss. Nothing seemed to be fair in life, so Heather decided to go home.

She crept up to the closet and quietly slipped into the back. Heather slept tightly around the yarn ball as if she would never see it again. Truly, she felt as if all life was draining from her body, inch by inch. Full and yet hungry, it was hard to explain the emptiness she felt, even to herself.

The next morning, Heather slipped out of the house with a heavy heart. As she wandered heavily down the path, she pulled away from the side where she left the dog. The old dog was still lying next to the garbage pile, with a peaceful look. A fitting memorial to their meeting, she thought.

Although they were controlling voices, Heather could sense the excitement and worry. Quietly, she slipped around the edge of the yard so she could see what the commotion was about. Heather positioned herself so she could hear the conversation without being noticed by everyone. There was a space between the garbage cans and the building that just fit her small body and put her in the shadows.

Two men dressed in blue, with lots of shiny things attached to the clothing, were questioning the little girl and her mother. Heather had seen some of these things before. The thing attached to the side made a loud explosive bang, just like they did back in the house. Heather was afraid of them, and the people that held them.

Memory flooded her mind of one afternoon in the early spring. To be awakened by a frightening explosion that almost blew away the old shed, was not pleasant. The two men and the lady were outside the shed, laughing at her as she shot out of the shed. Target practice is what they called it, and they continued shooting at the paper on the side of the shed. That was the last time Heather would ever sleep in the shed. Just as the old dog had found out, warm or not, they were humans, and it isn't safe.

The men had asked several questions about the strangers in the area. "Two men and a lady driving a late-model Buick, a silver one," said the first man. "One of the men was tall."

"I don't remember anyone with that description," said the little girl's mom. "I really haven't paid much attention lately. My little girl had been trying to make friends with the small cat we think belong to a friend of hers before she moved away. We've gotten her to at least eat something."

"Okay, Mrs. Skomp," the second man said, "but keep your eyes open. Call us immediately if you see or hear anything. These are dangerous people. They robbed a bank in Malone and shot one man. They were seen coming this way. We don't know if they are staying there, here, or not. The roadblocks didn't catch them, so we think they are staying low in the area."

"Britney," the one man said, "don't go off wandering in the woods today. We don't want anyone getting hurt with these people."

So her name was Britany, and her mom was Mrs. Skomp. At least she knew what to call these people now. At least, with names, they became true people, and not just part of the dream Heather had that filled her memory of long ago.

The strangers had hurt others, and these people didn't like it and thought they knew a way to stop them. Getting hurt wasn't part of Heather's plan either, but if you don't have any other place to live and only a few small crumbs to eat once in a while, what could you do? That's all Heather knew in this last year.

"How much did they take?" Mrs. Skomp asked.

"About $2,000," said the first man. "We were lucky. There was supposed to be a shipment of $1,000,000 for the payroll at Malone Metal, but the armored car had a flat tire that delayed it for two hours. They have been watching the operation for quite a while to know just when to move in."

Heather, in her small wisdom, knew that the people could be this mean. She had lived such a nightmare. This might explain some of what happened, and maybe there was a connection, but she would have to go home to find out. What could she do about it anyway? Heather didn't want to go home but knew that she must find out if the people in the house were the same people.

Heather felt the need to go home, having really nowhere else to turn. The people would at least leave for a few weeks. They had never stayed this long after a visit. Another thought ripped its way into Heather. If they left forever, there would never be any food, with or without pain.

At least now she had Britney to feed her, but she would never trust anyone. She supposed that things could get worse even if she didn't know how.

Heather edged around the building toward the woods. Just as Heather decided she should go back and check out her house to see if Jack and all of them were still there, Britney spotted her at the edge of the garage. Quickly, Heather ran past the trash and out into the alley. *Safe again*, she sighed and slowed down to a walk.

She felt funny today and good at the same time. She knew Britney was watching, and Britney knew she was watching. A chill of excitement ran up her back, like when a dog is pacing behind you, and yet, there was a new emptiness.

Heather turned off at the pass through the forest. Susan had come this way to a friend's house when she lived here, but Heather was never allowed to go. Only after Susan had gone, the gentleman who sold the house was gone, and there was no food—had Heather ventured off the area to where Britany's house stood.

Still, Heather felt a strange presence behind her. *Maybe another dog or cat was watching*, she thought. They wouldn't be any threat though, so Heather purred most of the way home.

With no malice in her heart, and no evil in her life, little did Heather know the path that lay ahead. Life is sometimes not fair to those who deserve happiness, and today was Heather's day.

*****

Britney knew today that Heather was alive. The tall man, who bought the house, came in the town for food sometimes, and he told her that Heather had been hit by a car and had died sometime last fall. She didn't need to check up on the cat, and his father needed all the quiet he could get. "Cranky old feller," he said. "Hates children. Wouldn't do to have someone come around makin' noise and scare him because of an old cat anyway."

Her mom was engrossed in talking to the policeman. Britney tried to tell her mom about the cat and the path. She knew Heather was alive. She needed to know what happened, and where she was living. She needed answers to so many questions that fluttered her head. *Why*, she thought, *can anyone neglect or abuse a beautiful cat like Heather?*

They had talked about abuse in school. She knew the signs. They had told her to tell someone, or talk to the person who was being abused. Maybe people could talk, not Heather. How could she tell? Maybe Britney could tell for her. But she had to know first.

Britney slipped from her mother's side into the backyard. "Be in the back with the cat," she called. As she entered the backyard, she knew that Heather had been spooked. She quietly followed Heather out to the alley where she saw her enter the yard to eat. Heather was just turning down the path to Susan's house. *Still there*, she thought quietly to herself so as not to scare Heather.

She followed in the distance, as quietly as a seven-year-old could. Once or twice, a twig snapped under her foot, and she had to stand like they play stone statues at school. It was hard, but Heather seemed to be in her own world today. Her attention was focused on something, or someone else.

Heather seemed to be less frightened than when she first spotted Britney. Britney didn't think her eyes told all the truth about seeing the outside of the cat. To see through the matted fur, even though the cat was a little more than skin and bones, Britney knew Heather.

She had called her mom to see, but her mom had only heard them talking about the cat. She had never really seen the cat, and then Heather was only a kitten. "You know, there are so many of those yellow tabbies around here. Could, could be any of them," her mother said.

Britney knew the path was long but didn't remember how long. She had only been here a few times before Susan left. It didn't make any difference; this was Susan's cat, and she knew her promise had to be good. When she called the cat's name, it seemed to frighten the cat more, like it was afraid of something, or memories. Britney saw the cat dash out into an opening, where the old house stood. It wasn't the same as when Susan was here. Britney knew that she would have to wait and see if anyone was around before she went to the house. It was a good thing she was careful and edged to the back of a tree, near the yard. She was as near as she could get, without being noticed. She saw the people that said that Heather was dead.

Britney crouched down to set on the ground and wait until they were asleep or left. She would go and retrieve the cat and take care of her, like she told Susan she would. But for now, she would have to wait. Having this responsibility was not easy.

Britney watched the men paint the car a dark blue. *That's dumb,* thought Britney. *The car didn't look like it needed painting. It was pretty silver. Maybe only the scratch on its side.* She waited as they removed the strips that held the papers on the window to keep the paint off.

Heather wandered over near the car. *No,* thought Britney. She didn't know what these people would do. Britney could almost not contain her love and care mixing at this pace. The man kicked Heather into the side of the shed, and Heather tried to get up and run. She wasn't fast enough to move out of the way of the man. He grabbed the tool from the ground and hit the cat hard. Britney cried softly and tears ran down in streaks from the dirt on her face.

The lady came out of the house to see what all the excitement was about. She seemed happy to see Heather lie there, with blood running from her small body. *I hate her,* thought Britney. *How can anyone…* She didn't finish her thoughts, for the new heaviness in her heart was making her sniffle, and she didn't want them to know what she had seen.

"I'll take care of this once and for all," one man said as he disappeared down the steps to the basement. Wonderment crossed Britney's face, but she remained quiet as a feather. She would go up when they left and find Heather. She, at least, would have a proper grave. Britney cried hard inside but remained vigil to the action outside the house.

"Can't leave tonight," the tall man said. "Paints too fresh. Anyone can smell it a mile away. Maybe tomorrow morning." With that, he disappeared inside the house.

Evening grew into the shades of night. The woman went inside with the other men. Britney never saw the man come from the basement, but she heard them talking upstairs, so she knew that all was clear, if she was very quiet and careful.

Britney crept quietly into the cellar, where she saw the man take Heather. It was hard for her eyes to focus in the dark. The cellar door squeaked, and Britney froze in fear. It didn't seem like they heard, but she wasn't going to stay long. Carefully, she began to search the basement and anything she could find. Just as she was almost ready to leave emptyhanded, her foot brushed the jars on the floor.

A crash echoed through the house that sounded like the giant in *Jack and the Beanstalk* could have landed in that cellar. The people appeared at the door before Britney could hardly move. The fear in her face, with the surprise in their face, brought an aura of impending doom.

The two men and the woman began screaming at each other as one man held on tight to the back of Britney's coat. "It's all your fault," screamed the shorter man. "If you had taken care of that stupid cat when I told you."

The taller man added quietly, "This is the girl that's always asking if I've seen it. Now what do we do?"

The woman was yelling, "Tie her up and leave her at the edge of the woods! Maybe someone will find the nosy little brat next spring. Keep things away from the house. We better get ready to leave and hurry up. Paint smell or not, someone will be out looking for her. And don't leave her where she can talk, understand?"

The tall man bit his lip hard. "We don't need this now. I'll get the car. You take care of her. Joe, get our things now." He then turned sharply to the other man's face. "You do have everything hidden, don't you? If we are found with the money, we won't have a chance."

Heather woke up, only to realize that her life was at the end of a threadbare string, ready to break. The edge of life neared as she knew she could no longer move. The dark abyss consumed her, and her life was as thin as the morning dew of summer.

The heavy dirt pressed on her body, squeezing Heather's life between her lips into a soft couple of "meows," and then the blackness of nothing.

Chapter 8

————— ❦ —————

The Way Home

Mrs. Skomp turned around after talking to the police to talk to Britney. At first, she thought maybe she had gone inside, or in the alley behind the house. Mrs. Skomp called to her and looked around the yard. Britney had disappeared so quickly; it frightened her. She called to the policeman who was ready to leave in the police car.

"Did Britney come that way?" Mrs. Skomp inquired.

Both the policeman and Britney's mom started looking for her. They searched the house, and the yard where she played. "Britney! Britney!" They called several times but no response. Britney never left the yard without her knowing. This began to get scary for Mrs. Skomp.

The policeman checked with the neighbors. No one had seen Britney outside her own yard. The afternoon was getting darker, and the evening light began fading into the night sky. The sky-blue haze turned into a dark-blue pool of air, and terror reigned in a mother's heart.

They called all her friends, and no one had seen the little girl. One of Britney's friends remembered the cat this morning. Britney had hoped it would come to stay. Her mother quickly pushed the memory of this morning back into focus. Britney had wanted to follow it, but she thought it might scare the cat away forever. Where would it have gone?

She remembered the path through the woods that Susan had taken when she visited. Her daughter and Susan were best friends until last year when Susan moved. Maybe the cat went home with Britney in pursuit.

They could try the path to Susan's house. The policeman called some other men to investigate and trace the path to the house, while others would go around and enter the woods from the opposite side, where the driveway entered from the road.

These people were still strangers after living there a year. No one knew much about them, but they didn't encourage anyone to be friendly, and the stories that Britney told about the cat scared them.

As the police car came up to the house, they pulled in slowly, looking around at all the possibilities. This was a mess. They must've had some money; the Buick was last year's model. They didn't use it for upkeep around here though.

As the two policemen got out of their car, they heard the fighting. There must've been several people involved here. There was supposed to be a husband and a wife living with her grandfather. This sounded like more than two people in a home spat. The voices began to mix into a blend of anger and fear.

The policeman eased up to the house and investigated the window, but there didn't seem to be anyone on the first floor. The voices came in clear around the basement door. The men crept quietly around to the basement door, just in time to hear the woman say, "Maybe someone will find this nosy little brat next spring. Keep things away from the house. We better get ready to leave and hurry up. Paint smell or not, someone will be looking out for her. And don't leave her where she can talk, understand?"

Through the crack in the basement door, he could see the man holding Britney. When the tall man told the other man to take care of her, he knew he couldn't wait any longer. He motioned to the policeman coming up the path to search the outside and back them up if there was trouble. They went through the door with a burst of energy fit for a lion. "What's happening here?" the first policeman asked.

Seeing the policeman keeping an eye on Britney, Jack dropped her to the ground and made a dive for the upstairs door. The second policeman blocked his way with the gun raised. "I don't think you want to do that," he retorted.

Joan seemed almost amazed that someone would step in and spoil her plan. Joe just stood there. "She came breaking in," he said. "I don't think this invasion of our privacy is necessary. Just take her and get out. I don't think she took anything, but she's the one who broke into our home."

Britney was in tears. "I just wanted my friend's cat, Heather." She explained that she came to find the cat that belonged to her friend who had lived here before. "These people told me that the cat had died, but I saw her. He killed her," Britney cried. "I saw him bring her down here, and I can't find her. I just want to bury her in a decent place," Britney wept.

Just then, a soft meowing came from behind the wall. "How did you get to that room?" the first policeman asked.

"You don't. There's no room over there. Must be outside," Joe said quietly.

Britney insisted that the other man brought the cat into the basement. "What does she know?" Jack sneered. "Just a dumb little girl who thought she saw a cat she knew. Could be anyone's cat."

"No!" Britney said. "Heather had the neatest black tip on her tail and the whitest beard on her chin. I know that was Heather."

The policeman leaned against the wall to listen and see if he could hear anything. The wall was still wet with plaster. "What did you plaster this for?" The policeman asked.

"Just cracking. The house needed some work done. You can surely see that," Joe snapped.

The first policeman began scraping the wet plaster away, and Jack squirmed, "Hey, you can't do that. This is our home."

"We can when we are in pursuit of criminals," the policeman snapped back.

As the policeman dug through the wall, his hand touched a tuff of fur. His hands flew into action and, quickly, he retrieved the small figure of a cat. Heather lay lifeless in his hand, and Britney fainted in tears.

The other policeman joined them in the basement as the first policeman went into action, placing the limp cat on the floor to see if there was any sign of life. He knew that he had heard the soft meows just a few seconds ago. Slowly as the policeman worked on Heather, she began to respond.

Soon, there were several more policemen and policewomen coming in. They had been searching in the woods. Some of them went back out to call for help. Both a doctor for Britney and a veterinarian for Heather were on their way.

The policeman searched the entire area where Heather had been. When the policeman pulled Heather from the wall, a sack for money marked "Malone Metal Payroll" was wrapped around her body.

After digging a small way further into the wall, they found the money in another sack. Three guns were resting underneath the sack.

"Don't touch them," the first policeman instructed. "Will call the crime lab to take this one apart. We will need the fingerprints."

"Just a regular family, right! Read them their rights and book them for robbery, kidnapping, and animal abuse," the first policeman said harshly. He was angry, angry that they had invaded the lives of so many, even Heather's.

Another policeman was searching outside when he spotted the silver paint on the hinge of the shed. The smell of fresh paint still hung heavy in the air. He walked over and lightly touched the car. He was right, fresh paint. He took a rag and dipped it in the paint thinner and wiped the outside of the fender, a silver streak shown through. "Glad this didn't set up any further," he said. As the two men and the woman were taken away, Britney broke into tears again—all the emotion of the afternoon had exhausted her. The doctor had arrived with her mother. He reassured them that she would be all right, but for tonight, she would be admitted to the hospital for rest and observation.

"Heather," the veterinarian said, "would take longer time, if at all, to recover." He didn't know how badly she had been damaged inside. He disappeared with the small bundle of fur wrapped in a warm blanket. He would phone Britney tomorrow. He knew it would be several days before all the tests would be returned from the lab and full recovery time could be determined. Everyone seemed angry that someone could do this to a child, or a helpless animal, like Heather.

Somewhere in the night, Heather slept peacefully in Susan's arms. The pain and agony of life were gone forever as she rested on a soft pillow covered in love, with wings of gossamer gold.

About the Author

Linda is a teacher media specialist/librarian, deaf interpreter, and storyteller. She loves working with children and adults in the educational setting. She loves reading young adult books. Writing seems to manifest itself in the middle of the night. Linda is thankful for the new technology that allows her thoughts to flow a little easier and faster to keep up with her brain. It also allows her to continue her learning, keeping her dependent on her children as her teachers. Her blended family of five boys, three girls, multiple grandchildren, and great-grandchildren are always a delight.

A few years back, Linda and her husband, with the help of their family, built a log cabin in the woods. They decided to do it by themselves and learned the skills needed to finish the house. She designed and created the stained glass in the kitchen with their names incorporated in the glass. It truly is one of a kind.

CPSIA information can be obtained
at www.ICGtesting.com
Printed in the USA
LVHW040127080621
689672LV00005B/230

9 781098 092375